9-15

DATE

10-7-15

WITHDRAWN

For Mike, with love, and Susie, who believed —L.M.R.

For my grandmother Luisa, who worked as a telegraph
operator in Ubaque, Colombia, in the 1930s —L.E.

Text copyright © 2015 by Lucy Margaret Rozier
Jacket art and interior illustrations copyright © 2015 by Leo Espinosa

All rights reserved. Published in the United States by Schwartz & Wade Books,
an imprint of Random House Children's Books, a division of Random House LLC,
a Penguin Random House Company, New York.

Schwartz & Wade Books and the colophon are trademarks of Random House LLC.

Visit us on the Web! randomhousekids.com
Educators and librarians, for a variety of teaching tools, visit us at RHTeachersLibrarians.com

Library of Congress Cataloging-in-Publication Data
Rozier, Lucy Margaret.
Jackrabbit McCabe and the electric telegraph / Lucy Margaret Rozier ; illustrator Leo Espinosa.
pages cm
Summary: Jackrabbit McCabe's unusually long legs have made him the fastest thing around, and he
uses his speed for everything from racing against horses to fetching the doctor, but when the electric
telegraph arrives in Windy Flats, Jackrabbit may have met his match.
ISBN 978-0-385-37843-7 (trade) — ISBN 978-0-385-37844-4 (glb) — ISBN 978-0-385-37845-1 (ebk)
[1. Speed—Fiction. 2. Telegraph—Fiction. 3. Tall tales.] I. Espinosa, Leo, illustrator. II. Title.
PZ7.R82746Jac 2015
[E]—dc23
2014010930

The text of this book is set in P22 Sherwood.
The illustrations were rendered in pencil and Adobe Photoshop.
Book design by Rachael Cole
MANUFACTURED IN CHINA
10 9 8 7 6 5 4 3 2 1
First Edition
Random House Children's Books supports the First Amendment and celebrates the right to read.

Jackrabbit McCabe & the Electric Telegraph

WRITTEN BY LUCY MARGARET ROZIER AND ILLUSTRATED BY LEO ESPINOSA

schwartz & wade books · new york

This here's the story of Jackrabbit McCabe, who was born to run. At birth, his legs were so long, they looped like a pretzel and his father had to add an extra axle to the baby carriage.

When he was a three-year-old, his mama
dressed him in long pants every morning,

but by noon his sock tops showed, and
by five o'clock, he was wearing shorts.

Little Jack chased whatever would run:
hogs, dogs, even his own shadow.

As he got older, he raced trains flying past his house in Windy Flats. For years, the engineers cheered him on. By the time he turned eighteen, he'd beat every stagecoach, antelope, and locomotive in the territory.

Perched on the edge of the Great Plains, the town of Windy Flats always counted on Jackrabbit's speed when a message had to get out fast— like to fetch ol' Doc Dobbins to patch up some ninny from the Double Dare Ya Club, who fell while climbing up St. Bertha's Church steeple.

Whenever the sky turned green and twisters bore down, Jackrabbit rounded up every wandering chick and child and plunked them safe back home.

On Sunday afternoons, he ran in horse races out at the county fairgrounds. Folks who knew Jackrabbit always bet on him to place first. Since he earned a piece of the pot, he made good money.

Then one day, something new came to Windy Flats:
the electric telegraph.

Out east, telegraph wires already crisscrossed the landscape, carrying messages quicker than the mail by using electricity. Each city and town connected by the wires had a telegraph and an operator who sent and received messages in Morse code, an alphabet of dots and dashes.

The first week the telegraph company showed up in Windy Flats, there was plenty of talk.

"I don't believe any newfangled contraption can carry a message faster than Jackrabbit," said Mayor Babble.

"Nor do I," said Judge Festoon.

The telegraph man overheard their boast and said, "How 'bout a race between your fella and this here electric telegraph? Sandy Bluff just got themselves an operator. That's pert near twenty-five miles, as the crow flies."

Of course, the mayor
had no trouble convincing
Jackrabbit to race.

"Why, yes, sir!" Jackrabbit said. "I can outrun anything!"

On the day of the big showdown, folks came from miles around. Windy Flats felt as festive as a flag-waving jubilee. A brass band played and Mayor Babble spoke.

Then the mayor carefully wrote down the same message on two slips of paper. He handed one to the telegraph man and the other to Jackrabbit.

To start the race, Judge Festoon

hollered so everyone could hear:

"On your marks, get set . . ."

A finger hovered just above the telegraph key.

Jackrabbit leaned way over with one foot already in the air.

"GO!"

Down went that telegraph key!

Off shot Jackrabbit McCabe!

Jackrabbit pumped his legs, kicking up storm clouds of dust. On the flat roof of the mercantile, children whooped and hollered as they watched him roar like a tornado down the road and out of sight.

The crowd held its breath.

In a few moments, a reply came clattering back as that telegraph key jumped and smacked all on its own.

The telegraph man quickly read the code and shouted:

"MESSAGE RECEIVED. STOP. SANDY BLUFF OPERATOR."

The crowd let its breath go in one great sigh. "Aw, shucks! Where's Jackrabbit McCabe?" they asked each other.

Well, sir, Jackrabbit ran in record time—nine and a half minutes to Sandy Bluff—but there was no brass band to welcome him, only a telegram tacked up on the door of the depot. It read:

TELEGRAM

As that fine statesman
and inventor
Benjamin Franklin
once said
energy and persistence
conquers all things stop

Mayor Babble
of Windy Flats

Jackrabbit pulled the mayor's message out of his pocket and read it with the Sandy Bluff telegraph operator. "Yep, they're the same. I guess I got beat."

Jackrabbit felt lower than a snake's navel.
He took a slow stagecoach ride home.

Meanwhile, Mayor Babble paced and thought. He was barely listening to the telegraph man's talk, till he heard, "Say, who's gonna be your telegraph operator?"

Suddenly, the mayor perked up. "What about Jackrabbit McCabe?" he said. "If his fingers are half as speedy as his long legs, we're in business."

And so, when Jackrabbit finally arrived back in Windy Flats, Mayor Babble was there to greet him. "Good news, my friend! How would you like to become the first telegraph operator of our fair city?"

Jackrabbit's shy grin quickly grew into a face-splitting smile.

He jumped up with a big "**Wahoo!**"

and ran six times around the town.

So Jackrabbit sent away for a Morse code book, and when it came, he practiced every minute. Before long, his fingers flew like a banjo player's, strumming that telegraph key. Day in and day out, he sent and received messages and, of course, hand-delivered telegrams in a flash.

He even teamed up with the local typesetter, who printed the news that came over that wire, linking Windy Flats to the whole entire country.

And who do you think delivered the newspaper every evening?

That's right—Jackrabbit, who could run through
every speck of town as fast as a squirrel hightails it up
a tree and, what's more, land a paper at every door.

Now I ask you, was there ever any fellow so all-fired expeditious as Jackrabbit McCabe?

Author's Note

In 1825, Samuel Morse, an American artist and inventor, missed his wife's last moments and her funeral because news of her sudden illness had taken several days traveling by horse from Connecticut, where they lived, to Washington, D.C., where he was painting a portrait.

In the early 1800s, scientists all over the world were racing to discover new uses for electricity. After that slow letter, Samuel Morse worked for twelve years to develop a way to send messages quickly over great distances, and in 1844, he created a telegraph system that was both practical and a commerical success. He and his partners also invented Morse code to use with the new device. After that, words could fly as fast as electricity.

To send a message, a telegraph operator tapped words in Morse code on a transmitting key, a lever that interrupted the electric current running through a wire. At the receiving end, these pulses were recorded as dots and dashes on a thin strip of paper. The operator there translated the code back into words, and the written message—called a telegram—was delivered.

By 1853, telegraph wires crisscrossed America from the Atlantic Ocean to the Mississippi River. Later, the lines went west with the railroads. After that, people learned of important events as soon as they happened!

Most of the "wires," as telegrams came to be called, were used by newspapers, railroads, governments, and stock markets. But they also helped folks share personal news, such as marriages, births, and deaths. Because people had to pay by the word, messages were generally short.

Telegraph service remained an efficient and widely popular means of communication through the middle of the twentieth century, until it was overtaken by newer technologies, such as the telephone.

Morse Code Key

A	.-		T	-
B	-...		U	..-
C	-.-.		V	...-
D	-..		W	.--
E	.		X	-..-
F	..-.		Y	-.--
G	--.		Z	--..
H	....			
I	..			
J	.---		1	.----
K	-.-		2	..---
L	.-..		3	...--
M	--		4	....-
N	-.		5	.....
O	---		6	-....
P	.--.		7	--...
Q	--.-		8	---..
R	.-.		9	----.
S	...		0	-----
Full Stop (period)	.-.-.-			
Question mark	..--..			

Using the key, translate this riddle from Morse code.

.... --- .-- / .. ... / .- / -. . .-- /

-.-. .- .-. / .-.- . -.- . / .----

.- -.-. -.- .-. .- -... -... .. -

..--.. / .. - / .-- ..- -. ... .-.-.-